To my Boys: Steve, Mitchell & Dean.

—J.J.

For my husband, David.

—S.M.

Book design by Jennifer West.
The illustrations in this book were rendered in watercolor and gouache.
Typeset in Engine.
Printed in Hong Kong.

Library of Congress Cataloging-in-Publication Data
Jordan, Jennifer
Albert goes to town / by Jennifer Jordan; illustrated by Shannon McNeill.
p. cm.
Summary: Albert's dream of driving a tiny car through his toy town is realized
with the help of a neighbor who is something more than he appears to be.
ISBN: 0-8118-0860-2
[1. Automobiles—Fiction. 2. Neighborliness—Fiction. 3. Magic—Fiction.]
I. McNeill, Shannon, 1970- ill. II. Title.
PZ7.J7626A1 1997   96-28720
[Fic]—dc20   CIP
AC

10 9 8 7 6 5 4 3 2 1

Distributed in Canada by Raincoast Books
8680 Cambie Street, Vancouver, British Columbia V6P 6M9

Chronicle Books
85 Second Street, San Francisco, California 94105

Website: www.chronbooks.com

Albert goes to Town

by Jennifer Jordan   Illustrated by Shannon McNeill

chronicle books · san francisco

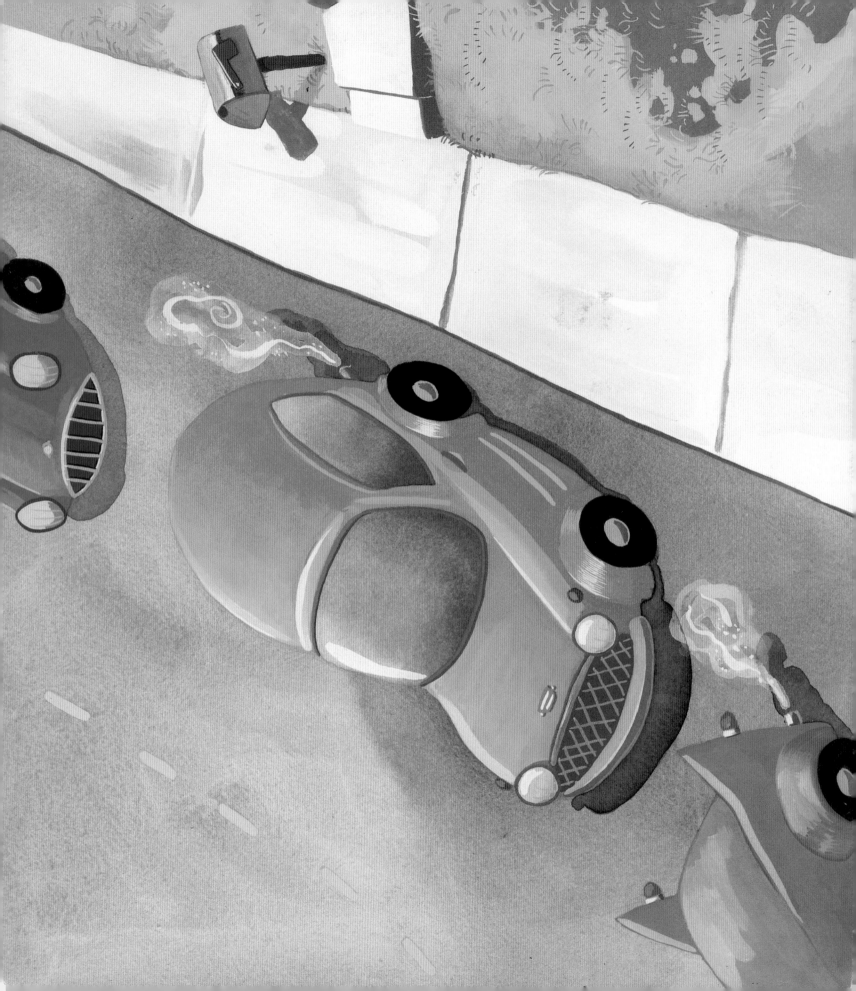

Albert loved cars. All cars.

He liked race cars and dune buggies,
police cars and vans.

Albert had dozens of toy cars in all colors and sizes.

He raced them and parked them.

He stacked and admired them.

But mostly he wished that he could climb inside
their tiny doors and drive them.

For Albert's last birthday, Mr. Appleby from next door had taken a large board and built an entire village on it.

Now Albert could steer his toy cars down a winding road, under a covered bridge, and past a green meadow.

There were black and white cows in the meadow, and little wooden apples in the apple trees. And, in the town, all of the houses looked like those on Albert's own block.

There was even one like Mr. Appleby's.

Mr. Appleby lived in a tiny yellow house with a huge overgrown garden. In back, his old work shed was filled with tools, and scraps of wood waiting to be turned into something wonderful.

A birdhouse.

A windowbox.

Toys. Mr. Appleby loved to make toys.

One day, Albert tapped on the window of the shed. Mr. Appleby opened the door. "How's Albert today?" he said.

"All right," Albert sighed. "Thank you for the town you made for my cars."

Mr. Appleby smiled. "You are very welcome, my friend," he said. "Just see that you enjoy it!"

"Oh I do! I drive my cars around and around. I think it would be a wonderful place to visit." Albert paused. "I wish that I could drive there myself," he whispered, "that's what I truly wish."

Instead of his wish, Albert got the flu.

For nearly a week he had to stay in bed and get plenty of rest. After his fever had gone, he was allowed to sit in a big lawn chair in his backyard. He watched Mr. Appleby going in and out of his work shed.

Albert waved.

Mr. Appleby waved back.

"I have a cold!" Albert shouted.

"I know!" Mr. Appleby hollered back. "As soon as you are well enough, come on over. I've got a surprise for you."

In the morning, after promising not to tire himself on his very first day out, Albert hurried next door. As he approached the work shed, he heard Mr. Appleby whistling.

Albert peeked into the window.

There, in the middle of the floor, stood the most beautiful little wooden car. Just Albert's size.

It was a convertible with spoked wheels and one little seat.

It was polished so it glowed.

Albert burst through the door
sending a cloud of sawdust through the sunbeams.

"Is this it?" Albert cried, "Is this my surprise?"

"This here?" Mr. Appleby said, pointing to the car.
"No, no. This isn't the surprise."

The smile dropped from Albert's face like a stone.

"Oh, the car is for you," Mr. Appleby added,
"but the real surprise is outside."

Albert eagerly helped Mr. Appleby push the little car outside.

"Get in and try her out," Mr. Appleby said.

Albert opened the door and slid onto the seat. He curled his fingers around the smooth wooden steering wheel and turned it back and forth. It was just like a real car! There were buttons and levers in all the right places.

There were even gas and brake pedals on the floor.

Mr. Appleby smiled and reached inside the car.

Right where it should be was a tiny wooden key. He turned it.

The car made a **clickety-clack** sound and Albert felt it spring to life around him.

Mr. Appleby pointed toward an opening in a big honeysuckle bush.

"Take her for a spin," he said.

Cautiously, Albert stepped on the gas pedal. The car **lurched** forward a few feet. Albert quickly lifted his foot, and the car rolled to a stop.

Mr. Appleby shouted,

"Give her some gas and let her fly!"

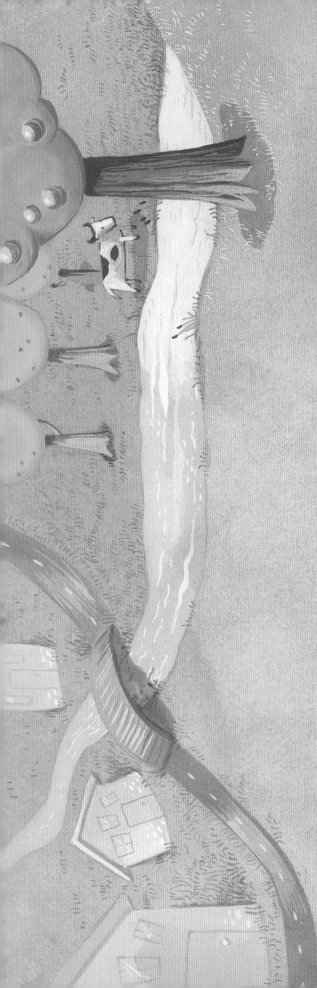

Albert pushed hard on the pedal and ducked his head.
He crashed through the sweet smelling bushes, **bumpety crack.**

When he opened his eyes, he found himself cruising along the street in front of his house. He passed Mr. Appleby's house and the others on his block. As he turned the corner he came upon a covered bridge that he didn't remember ever seeing before.

Up ahead, the road was lined with shiny green grass and trees. Then he passed a large meadow. "Moo!" Albert shouted to a herd of black and white cows.

As he drove, a perfect red apple plopped into his lap.

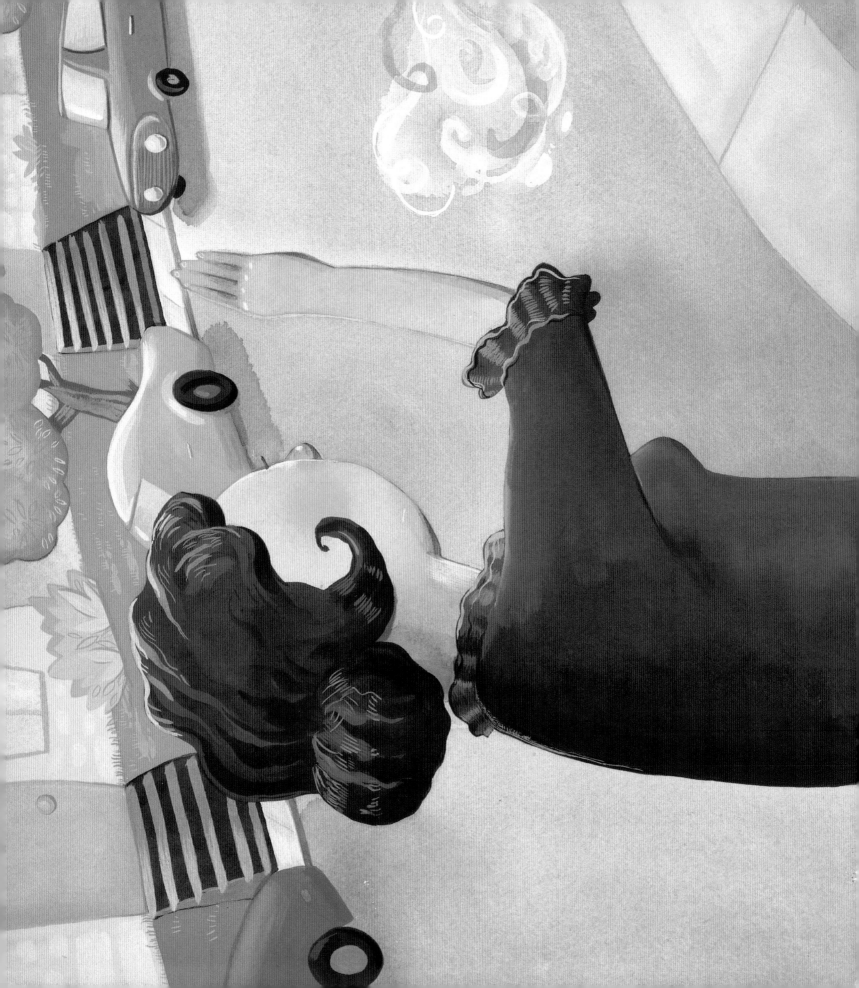

Around the next curve,
Albert spotted his house. He noticed
his mother standing on the front porch.
"Hi mom!" Albert called. "Look at me! I'm driving!"

Down the block, Mr. Appleby's cat was halfway up a tree
with the Barker's dog, Ralph, close behind.

Albert **zoomed** past, going faster and faster.
The wind **rushed** by his ears and ruffled his hair.

Albert passed cars and trucks of all kinds lined up carefully along the road.
But none were moving. They had no drivers.

"Hi!" Albert shouted to his mother as he turned onto his street again.

Again, she seemed not to notice him. In fact, no one seemed to notice much of anything. Each time Albert passed, everyone was exactly the same as they were before—stiff as wooden soldiers. Even Mr. Appleby's cat was no further up the tree, and Ralph was no closer to catching him.

"Mom?" No reply. Albert raised his voice. "Mom!"

"Albert!" her voice called back.

Albert smiled and turned quickly into Mr. Appleby's driveway. As he headed up the drive, he could hear his mother calling his name again. Albert hurried toward the garden. He drove right through the lower branches of the big honeysuckle bush and **bounced** along the path to the work shed.

The clatter of the engine suddenly stopped.

"Albert!" His mother's voice was loud and clear as she strode across the lawn. Mr. Appleby hurried out of the shed.

"Mom!" Albert cried, "Look at the car Mr. Appleby made just for me! I can drive it all by myself!"

He turned the wooden key back and forth.

He stepped on the gas pedal, **clack, clack.**

Nothing happened.

Albert's mother walked over to the car.
"It's a wonderful toy," she said as she reached
for his hand, "but it's time for you to get
some rest now."

Albert looked at Mr. Appleby in disbelief.
As he stood, a tiny red bead fell from
his lap and rolled down the drive.

"Hey, it's one of the apples
from my wooden town!"

The three stood and watched as the little wooden bead **bounced** out of sight.

"Never mind, Albert," said Mr. Appleby, "there's plenty more where that came from. Drive over any time and get another."

Albert grinned from ear to ear as he got back in behind the wheel of the beautiful wooden car. His mother gave a push and the two of them bumped across the lawn. As Albert turned to wave, he saw Mr. Appleby reach through the bottom branches of the honeysuckle bush. Out came a shiny red apple.

"Good-bye!" Albert hollered.

Mr. Appleby winked and took a big bite.